Florence The Data Scientist
and
Her Magical Bookmobile

By Ryan Kelly

Illustrated by Mernie Gallagher-Cole

For Beatrice, my smallest best friend.
May you never stop being curious about
the world around you.

Emily, Rebecca, Kate, Steve, Jenny, Kelli, Dinesh, and Eric:
thank you for helping make this book possible.

"Wow! This is such a hap-hap-happy day!"
Beatrice hummed putting her things away.
She opened her bag, took her Jupyter out.
Here is the notebook I can't live without!"

Beatrice liked to do four different things.

She loved reading and science, dragons, and swings.

"My Jupyter notebook will help me a bunch!"

she said to her Mom who just brought up her lunch.

"Oh Mom, I love you! You're so good to me!"

Beatrice said with a hug lovingly.

As she crunched and she munched, she suddenly heard . . .
A jingling and jangling, and then it occurred!
A colorful truck drove right down her street,
clinging and clanging a musical beat!
A magical bookmobile? Beatrice thought,
excited to see all the books that it brought!

A curious person appeared at the door.

She opened the window and pulled out a drawer.

She reached deep inside and pressed buttons and keys

creating a storefront with great expertise.

Beatrice wondered who Florence might be
as children rushed over and lined up with glee.
Florence seemed friendly. She made the kids laugh,
Beatrice observed, creating a graph.

"You may each take a turn," Florence declared.
"By answering three questions I have prepared."
Sofia was first. She jumped up and down,
excited to answer, she wiggled around.

Florence began and said, "Please tell me now,
have you ever owned a dog, cat, or cow?
Question two. Do you like books that are real,
or do make-believe books have more appeal?

The very last question, would you rather be
remarkably strong or fly high and free?"
Sofia was shy, but she expressed her reply,
"I have a cat. I like make-believe, and fly!"

"Good job!" Florence said, "Wait here, I'll be back!"
Soon she returned with a book in a sack.
"This book is for you, Sofia my dear."
"Yippie!" she shouted, quite pleased and sincere.

She rushed to a bench and opened her book.

A few pages later... **POOF!**

The ground shook!

A beautiful unicorn had just appeared!

They rode off together as all the kids cheered.

Beatrice continued to watch and record. Analyzing data, she never got bored.

Jose was next, he was ready to begin.

He answered the questions with speed and a grin.

"A cow, real, and strong!" Jose said aloud.

"I have just the book!" Florence told the crowd.

With great delight, he thanked her for the book.

Then Jose sat down to take a good look.

His eyes grew wide as he started to read,
and in just a few pages . . . **POOF!**
Magic – guaranteed!
An eagle escaped from the book to the sky
encircling his head, then landed nearby.

Moxie and Izzie stepped up for their turn,

and Florence was anxious to hear what she'd learn.

"I like make-believe stories. I own a greyhound.

And I'd like to fly! How does that sound?"

"That sounds mighty good!" Florence said to Izzie.

"I'm so glad you all came! I like being busy!"

Moxie, her brother, was pleased to come along,
said, "I have a dog and I want to be strong!
And I like make-believe the very best of all.
May I have a magic book, even though I'm small?"

Beatrice recorded each answer she heard,
carefully watching as each event occurred.

"You sure do!" said Florence, returning right quick,

while Moxie and Izzie awaited her pick.

Each meant for their age and similar in style,

Florence gave them their books, which made them each smile.

Anxious to read them, they both peered inside!
After just a few pages... **POOF!**
"Magic!" they cried.
Two friendly dragons appeared from each tale.
They played and they laughed, taking off down the trail.

Then the next girl in line stepped up and said,

"Make-believe books are the ones that I've read.

Plus, I have a cat and want to

fly in the breeze!

May I have a magic book?

It's my turn,

pretty please?"

Florence presented a pop-up
book to read,
then just minutes later,
a unicorn was freed!

"Wow!" said Beatrice, continuing to record.
"Mom! You should see this! It can't be ignored!"
She studied the data, tried to decide;
analyzed numbers, each one side by side.
Was there an answer? What did it mean?
She looked at the data. Was there a routine?

"What is it Honey?" her mom said at last.

"It's so amazing! I've been having a blast!

The magic bookmobile, right on our street

makes animals from stories, then - **POOF!**

It's so neat!

They just come to life. You should see it! It's true.

I've watched from the start all the way through!"

"Keep up the good work. You'll figure it out!"
said Beatrice's mom without any doubt.
So, that's what she did. She watched and she waited.
As each took a turn, Beatrice calculated.

There were more questions. . .

There were more books. . .

There were more animals. . .

And lots of surprised looks. . .

It was all so exciting . . .

"But what does it mean?"

her mom managed to ask somewhere in between.

Beatrice smiled. She'd been thinking quite hard.

When her mom asked the question, she caught her off-guard.

"What kind of animals?" her mom inquired.

"Eagles, unicorns, and dragons were acquired!"

"I recorded the data, saw a pattern or two.
She asked the same questions, so that was a clue.
It depends on the answers to see what you'll get—
An eagle, a unicorn, or dragon - it's set."

"Did you see a pattern or some recognition?"
asked her mom suggesting any repetition.
Beatrice nodded, as she was quite polite.
"Some are so tricky. They don't come out right!"

"Think through the data. Don't let yourself get tricked.

Visualize the answer. What do you predict?"

"I'm sure I want a dragon, but I also know,

I must find the answers to see how it will go."

"It looks like Florence is about to hit the road."

"Oh no! My brain feels like it's going to explode!"

"Take a deep breath," her mom tried to say

as Beatrice frowned and analyzed away.

"Yikes!" cried Beatrice as she ran down the stairs
reflecting, assessing, and forecasting her errs.
"I've got it!" she squealed, without any doubt.
Now she was ready to try it all out!

"Please, wait! May I please get a book from you too?"

"Most surely my dear, I have one for you!
I noticed that you have been watching all day,
but now it's your turn to answer away!"

Florence began and said, "Please tell me now,
have you ever owned a dog, cat, or cow?
Question two. Do you like books that are real,
or do make-believe books have more appeal?
The very last question, would you rather be
remarkably strong or fly high and free?"

"I think make-believe books are really first rate.
I have a dog, and to fly would be great."

"Inside of this book, I hope you will find
wonderful treats – the data science kind!

"You worked very hard to analyze and record.
I thought only I knew how choice leads to reward."

They waved to each other as the truck pulled away,
and Beatrice sat down to read without delay.
Then . . .

POOF!

The dragon peeked out, licking her cheek,

smiling, and laughing, and making her shriek!
Then . . . **POOF!**

The dragon was out, and they started to prance.

This young data scientist did a happy data dance!

You can be a Data Scientist, too!

What is a Data Scientist?

A data scientist is someone like Florence who collects, analyzes, and makes decisions using large amounts of data, or information. Just like an astronomer studies the stars and planets, or a marine biologist studies ocean animals and plants, a data scientist studies data—all kinds of it!

What is data?

Data is information about most anything! You can have data on how many books are borrowed from the library every day, what the temperature is outside, how many stuffed animals you collect, and information relating to the x-ray images taken by a doctor.

What is data used for?

Data scientists can use data about things that have happened in the past to build a model to predict what may happen in the future.

How do they do that?

They begin their work by asking questions like Florence did – lots and lots of questions – to gather information. In the beginning, they may not even know what data will be the most important, so they record all of it very carefully.

Next, they use their math and reasoning skills to look for patterns, just like Beatrice did. You can do it, too, using notebooks, tables, and graphs. When there is a lot of data, computers can do millions of calculations for you.

With all that knowledge, they can create some really powerful models to predict the future. These predictions can help identify and cure diseases, catch criminals, create self-driving cars, and much more!